Oracle

Oracle

Alex Van Tol

Orca currents

ORCA BOOK PUBLISHERS

Library and Archives Canada Cataloguing in Publication

Van Tol, Alex
Oracle / Alex Van Tol.
(Orca currents)

Issued also in electronic formats.
ISBN 978-1-4598-0133-2 (BOUND).—ISBN 978-1-4598-0132-5 (PBK.)

I. Title. II. Series: Orca currents
PS8643.A63073 2012   jc813'.6   C2012-902568-2

First published in the United States, 2012
Library of Congress Control Number: 2012938209

Summary: Owen sets up an anonymous blog to influence a girl at school.

*Orca Book Publishers is dedicated to preserving the environment and has
printed this book on paper certified by the Forest Stewardship Council®.*

Orca Book Publishers gratefully acknowledges the support for its
publishing programs provided by the following agencies: the Government
of Canada through the Canada Book Fund and the Canada Council for the Arts,
and the Province of British Columbia through the BC Arts Council
and the Book Publishing Tax Credit.

10% of author royalties will go toward supporting the work of Kids Help Phone.

Cover photography by Thinkstock

ORCA BOOK PUBLISHERS
PO Box 5626, Stn. B
Victoria, BC Canada
V8R 6S4

ORCA BOOK PUBLISHERS
PO Box 468
Custer, WA USA
98240-0468

www.orcabook.com
Printed and bound in Canada.

15 14 13 12 • 4 3 2 1

Chapter One

I can't help it. She's beautiful. I have to stare.

My love is like to ice and I to fire.

The words from that Renaissance guy's poem spool around in my head in a repeating loop. Mr. Schmidt would be proud that I remembered something from his class last year.

1

Poems don't usually make a lot of sense to me. But this one did. It was so true. The harder this poor guy loved the girl, the colder she got. He can't figure out why he can't melt her one little bit when he burns for her.

I totally get that. Looking at her stony perfection, I don't think I could melt Kamryn Holt's heart in a million years.

But that doesn't mean I can't try.

Maybe I'll ask her to go to the dance with me.

Huh. Right.

Maybe when pigs fly.

When the bell rings, my daydream ends and another screamingly dull social studies class is over. People fling their books into their bags and charge out the door.

It's lunch, and finally it's nice enough to sit outside.

By the time I make it through the crowded doorway, Kamryn is sitting at her usual place on the concrete wall. She is surrounded by other girls.

Even if I wanted to ask her to the dance, there's no way I could do it in front of that crowd. How do guys ever get anywhere with girls when all girls do is huddle together like a bunch of ducks?

The wall is a popular spot for the eights and nines. The sevens sit at the picnic tables. The sixes run around on the playground, screaming and pushing each other like demented toddlers. The senior students usually go to McDonald's or Starbucks for lunch.

I stroll toward the wall. I take a seat a few feet down from the girl gaggle. I pull my iPod from my backpack. Mason spots me and heads across the grass in my direction.

I unwind my headphones and take a package of cookies from my lunch.

Scratch that. The cookies *are* my lunch. I've been raised on Oreos and

Chips Ahoy ever since my mom declared she was done making lunches. That was two years ago.

Mason drops his pack and plops down. "I hate Prost's class," he says. "He's so picky."

"Got your essay back?" I ask, glancing at him. Kamryn is exactly in my line of sight. I should thank Mason for sitting in the perfect spot.

Mason nods. "He killed it," he says. "I mean, who cares if I spell *dumb* without the b? It's *silent.* Who remembers to add silent letters anyway?"

I shrug. "People who passed grade two?" I pop an Oreo into my mouth.

"Weren't you the one who failed grade two?" he retorts.

"I *taught* it, bro."

Mason laughs. "Hey, you coming over tonight? I finally got *Naruto Shippuden* for my Xbox. You can let my ninja kick your ninja's butt."

"I have to stick around to help Ms. Hamilton with math tutorial after school," I say. "But I'll come after dinner if I don't have too much homework."

"Math help? Seriously?" Mason says. He unwraps a tasty-looking sandwich. "You're such a keener, O-man."

"She totally cornered me," I protest. "What am I going to say? No?"

"Yeah, that's exactly what you should say." Mason takes a big bite of his sandwich. My attention drifts to where Kamryn sits with Becca farther down the wall.

Giggling, the two girls stand. I chew faster once I see them moving my way. I don't want to have sticky brown teeth if Kamryn stops to talk.

Like she ever would. She knows I exist, but that's about as deep as our relationship goes.

I swallow and take a slug of water, swishing. Why didn't I pick the vanilla Oreos this morning?

Kamryn and Becca move toward the stairs, talking. My heart speeds up when Becca stops in front of us. For one agonizing second I think she's going to talk to me. Which might be good, because it would open a conversation with Kamryn. It also might not be good, because I might end up looking like a freak with gooey black teeth.

Turns out I don't have to worry. Neither of them notice my existence.

Becca drops her bag and leans over to retie her sandal. It's one of those complicated ones with the ties that criss-cross up the leg. It looks like it might take her awhile.

I keep my eyes down and listen.

"God, you should *so* not borrow these sandals for the spring dance, Kam," Becca says. "This is the third time today I've had to retie them."

"Yeah, but they look hot," Kamryn says. "Isn't that what matters?"

"True, it is," says Becca. "So? Are you going to talk to him at the dance?"

"Yes, and I'm so freaked out about it!"

"Why?"

"I'm still trying to figure out what to say," Kamryn says.

"Think he's noticed you?"

"Totally!" Kamryn exclaims. "You were right there when he was staring at me at the game last Friday. He, like, couldn't take his eyes off me."

"But he's in high school, Kam." Becca finishes her knot with an extra tug and straightens.

Kamryn's after someone older?

"So? He's not *that* much older, Bex. Grade ten? Hello? That's only two years. Actually, less," she adds. "His birthday is in October and mine's in March, so we're really only, like, sixteen months apart."

At the mention of *grade ten* and *October*, my stomach gives a little twist.

The next thing she says sends it into full seizure mode.

"It's meant to be, Bex. Think about it. Kyle and Kamryn? How perfect is that? How do we *not* belong together?"

Kyle?

I try to swallow. Beside me, Mason crumples up his wax paper. He reaches for his Coke.

Kyle?

"Okay, so maybe you belong together," says Becca. "But how are you going to *get* together?"

"That's where I need a plan. And a superhot outfit," Kamryn says as they move off.

My stomach gives another sickening turn as it all sinks in. This is so wrong. So totally wrong.

That grade-ten guy she's talking about? The one named Kyle?

He's my brother.

Chapter Two

The girl I am desperately crushing on is in love with my big brother.

How am I supposed to be okay with this?

The guy's a jerk. I wish I could go up to Kamryn and tell her flat out that the good-looking basketball star she thinks is so fantastic has broken at least a dozen hearts in the last ten months alone. I wish I could tell her he's a waste of space.

And that last guy she was with? Segal? He was a jerk too.

I wish I could tell Kamryn that she should give me a chance. I'd treat her like a princess.

Yeah, right. Like I'd ever have the guts to tell her something like that. Like she'd ever listen to me anyway.

My afternoon crawls along. The seconds tick by even slower when I remember I'm supposed to start that stupid math tutoring today.

The tutorial hour passes like a turtle walking backward through cement. Perfect squares and square roots and ratios. But at 3:40, I'm finally free.

I skip the bus and decide to walk home. I need to think. I need to give my brain time to obsess about Kamryn trying to get together with my brother. My loser, jerk brother. He looks great on the outside, but he uses people to get what he wants.

How can I get what *I* want?

I want to get Kamryn to like me instead of Kyle. But how do I do that?

This requires serious thinking. And serious thinking requires serious fuel. I double back half a block to the 7-Eleven. I buy a carton of milk and a bag of black licorice. The combination grosses all my friends out. But it works, especially when applied just before massive brainpower output. It's gotten me through at least seven major exams, one prepared speech and a really confusing breakup with a girl who was way better than me at talking in circles.

I take my sugar overdose outside with me and sit down on a parking block. I have to think. I have to come up with a plan to make Kamryn realize not only that Kyle is a weenie, but that she should spend her time with me instead.

Plan A: I kill Kyle outright. Then I won't have to think about him for the rest of my life. No more awards banquets. No more driving around to weekend tournaments. No more pictures of my grinning brother caught up in one-armed hugs with sports celebrities.

I go very still as I think about this for a moment. A warm feeling comes over me. I stop chewing and lose myself in the thought of a Kyle-free world.

I blink.

No. I can't kill Kyle.

The warm feeling goes away. The familiar knot of irritation settles back into place in my chest. I sigh.

Plan B: I go right up to Kamryn and tell her she's hot and that I want her in my world. I say that Kyle is a doofus who leaves poo streaks in his Jockeys. I tell her I am clean, kind and full of love.

Somehow I don't think that plan is going to fly.

Something sneaky might work though. What if I could somehow communicate the same basic information to Kamryn without her knowing it's from me?

I chew through three more pieces of licorice while I brainstorm various options. I remind myself that anything goes when you're brainstorming. Stupid ideas included.

Write an article in the newspaper about how Kyle sucks. (Who reads the newspaper?)

Make an announcement on the radio about how Kyle sucks. (Really? Stupid.)

Buy ad time on TV and make an ad about how Kyle sucks. (Really? Really *really?*)

Make a YouTube video about how Kyle sucks. (Too revealing.)

Write Kamryn a note about how Kyle sucks. (Possible. But she'll know it's from someone who's jealous. And even if a single note was enough to convince her—which it wouldn't be—how do I take the next step of showing her that I'm the right guy?)

Write Kamryn a poem about the kind of guy who's perfect for her. (This is more promising. Girls go for poems. Don't they?)

No, not a poem. Not a note. A conversation. There has to be a way to engage Kamryn in some sort of back-and-forth. Then I can reel her in slowly. Get her to fall for me, without giving away my identity.

At least, not until I've got her, hook, line and sinker.

I think about my options here.

Post on a blog that she reads and get her interested enough to leave a comment? Could I start the conversation that way?

But how do I know what she reads? Her Facebook page isn't public, so I can't see her Likes. I don't know which websites she reads. Which means I have to catch her attention—and keep her interested—with something new.

A website where…where what? What would interest an eighth-grade girl enough to keep her checking every day? Shoes? Clothes? Makeup? I don't know anything about that stuff.

Huh. What about relationships? I can probably make that stuff up.

Okay. Plan C.

Set up an anonymous blog and write a bunch of posts about relationships at my school. Write the blog like someone who can see the future. Get people excited about it so that lots of them read it. And come to depend on it for advice.

And then, through the blog, I'll convince Kamryn that I'm a better option than Kyle.

I look around, excited. I think this could work!

I need to think of a name.

I think about the Big Idea, like teachers always tell you to do. I need a great name that tells people what kind of blog it is. It needs to say that it's a place to go for advice on relationships, looking into the future. The name should make people think of a crystal ball, but with more practical suggestions.

I need something catchy, easy to say and easy to remember.

Wizard? Nah. Wizards create magic. They don't give advice.

Muse? No. I'm not going to be inspiring people.

Mystic? That sounds like I should be handing out green tea and crystals.

I play with the words for a few more minutes, until the perfect one arrives. When it finally drops into my mind, I get one of those powerful full-body shivers.

Oracle.

I grin suddenly and spook a small child walking through the parking lot. He stares.

I stand and fire my milk carton into the garbage.

Let the games begin.

Chapter Three

I settle into my chair and open up my laptop. I set up my blog name. *Oracle.*

I set up the About page with a picture of an ancient temple. Then I write my bio. I'm careful to keep it anonymous while still letting it be known that I'm a member of the school community.

By day, I'm a student at LaMontagne. You know me, but I know you even better.

Call me the Oracle. Here's where you'll find direction in life and love at LaMontagne.

I pause. Yeah, but how do I give that direction? How do I get people to leave comments so that I can get the conversation started?

I start typing again. *Want to find your soul mate? Wondering how to make that cute guy or girl fall head over heels for you? Need tips to get that first conversation started? Ask the Oracle.*

I decide to write a post and then answer it with a comment. Then it'll look like someone has already asked the Oracle questions.

So, then, I'll post about…what?

My shoulders slump. I've hit a wall. I can't just make up stories about the people at LaMontagne. I can't use names. I can't write about my own situation, because I'll give myself away.

I type *relationship advice* into Google. Twenty-nine million hits! I dive in and read Q&As on different websites. After a few minutes of reading, I find a question that will work perfectly. *My boyfriend and I have been going out for five months. We used to talk all the time. Now he doesn't return my calls. He says he's just busy with soccer season. Should I keep calling him?*

I don't even need to read the answer to know that the guy's trying to tell her it's over.

This is so easy! I can basically copy and paste questions and answers. This won't take me very long at all.

I click on *New Post*. My grin slides off my face when the hole in my plan becomes obvious.

I can't keep posting random questions and answering them. If I want this thing to get off the ground, I have to find a way to get *other* people to submit questions.

Which is impossible, since no one knows the blog exists.

I sigh in frustration. How can this be so complicated?

I stand up, suddenly needing to get out of here. I slip on a hoodie and stuff my phone into my pocket. I grab my skateboard and a couple of bucks for a Slurpee.

When the going gets tough, I go for a skate.

I'm still stumped when I roll into the 7-Eleven.

I kick up my board with one hand and grab for the door handle with the other.

I yank the door open without looking. From inside the store comes the sound of girls chattering.

By the time I feel the weight of someone leaning on the other side of the door, it's already halfway open. I stagger backward as someone crashes into my chest.

"*Oof!*" My breath punches out of me. Reflexively, my arms come up. I drop my board. It clatters to the concrete. Cold slushy stuff hits my arm and stomach. I find myself in an unexpected hug with I'm-not-sure-who. The Slurpee on my shirt soaks through, freezing my stomach against whoever I'm now holding in my arms.

The chatter turns to gasps.

"Oh my god! Kamryn!" a girl's voice shrieks. "Are you okay?"

Kamryn? Oh *crap*.

I shrink back like I've been burned. In my clumsy scramble to push our bodies apart, my hands land on something soft. Really soft.

Kamryn squeals in outrage.

I realize in horror where my palms have landed.

"Sorry! I'm sorry!" I shout. I snatch my hands away, upsetting her balance again.

She stumbles forward, and our heads bonk. Oh my god, could this get any worse?

Dana grabs for Kamryn to steady her. She narrows her eyes at me. "Look where you're going, you *idiot*," she sneers.

The air is filled with exclamations as Kamryn's friends flutter around her. They throw me dirty scowls.

Her balance finally restored, Kamryn glares at me. If she never noticed me before, she'll sure remember me now. She smooths her hair back, her chin jutting. "Don't you *ever* touch me again," she hisses. Her glare could break apart diamonds.

"I wasn't..." I fumble. "I didn't mean..." I shake my head and take a step back.

My foot lands on my skateboard. The wheels engage, sliding easily along the concrete. I go sprawling backward. My leg overcompensates, pushing the board forward. Horrified, I watch as it shoots out from under me and slams into Kamryn's shin. She gasps and clutches at her leg.

Apparently, it *can* get worse.

Kamryn's eyes narrow into sharp slits of glittering green. She is just getting ready to slay me when the door behind her opens.

"Owen. Hey." I look up to see Hannah, the president of the student council. She looks surprised but wary. "Everything okay?"

Kamryn straightens and glances at Hannah. She doesn't say whatever she'd planned to say to me. Not in front of Hannah, at least. Everyone likes Hannah. She's always nice, always honest, but funny and cool at the same time. People want her to think well of them.

Kamryn gives me a final glare. Her friends close around her, and they move away, talking. Kamryn is waving her hands and shaking her head. I'm sure she's telling everyone how stupid I am for opening the door.

Never mind that she was leaning on it, not looking where she was going.

Hannah watches the receding group. "What was that all about?"

I shake my head. "She crashed into me when I opened the door," I say. "And now she's got a full hate-on for me."

Hannah sighs. "I wouldn't worry about it too much, Owen," she says. "It's pretty hard to stay in Kamryn's good books."

She sticks a hand out, and I take it. "Thanks," I say. She pulls me up, and I dust off my butt. My shirt is cold and wet, and it sticks to my stomach. Gross.

But as I look at Hannah, it hits me. I think I've found a solution to my problem.

Chapter Four

"Tell me again why you're doing this?" Hannah asks.

I upend my board and grab it by the trucks. We climb the front stairs of my house. "'Cause. It'll be fun." I jiggle my key in the old brass lock. The door swings open, and I step into the entryway.

Hannah doesn't follow. She stays on the doorstep, arms folded. "Owen."

Only Hannah has that way of saying my name. "Flash mobs are fun. Parasailing is fun. But writing a relationship blog? This doesn't sound like you. What's going on?"

Crap. She's not buying it. She'll laugh if I tell her the real reason behind the Oracle. Especially after what she witnessed today.

I shrug. "I want to see how many people I can get to read it." I motion for her to come in. She stands in the doorway, stubbornly.

I sigh and push her out of the way so I can close the door. Hannah's not someone most people can push out of the way. But I can. We've been friends since our mothers met at baby music class thirteen years ago. I've seen Hannah barf all down her best dress. She's seen me pee my pants. Twice.

Hannah furrows her dark brows. "You want to see how many people read it?"

she repeats. "Really? Owen, when was the last time you wrote more than ten words in a row? What's with the sudden urge to host an entire"—she looks for the right word—"gossip blog for our school?"

I put my arm around her shoulders. "I don't plan to do it all alone," I say. "You're going to help me."

"I'm going to help you?" She looks at me like I'm speaking Finnish. "I haven't agreed to anything."

"Ah, but you're brilliant, Hannah," I say, laying it on thick. "Your ideas are way better than mine. Your research skills are tops. Plus, you're funny."

Never mind that I'm too lazy to make the blog happen by myself. I *need* her help to get it up and running.

I head for the kitchen. I don't want to appear desperate. I'll lose ground if she thinks it matters too much.

She follows me into the kitchen, her arms still crossed. I take two packages of cookies out of the cupboard and hand one to her. She shakes her head and takes an apple from the fruit bowl instead.

"Are you going to tell me what this is *really* all about?" she says, polishing her apple on her jeans.

I sigh. Hannah can't be dodged. She knows me way too well. I go straight to the heart of it. "Kamryn's in love with my brother."

"So?"

"Well, Kyle's a jerk. You know that."

"I do know that," says Hannah. "But I don't see what a blog has to do with it." She takes a bite of apple.

"I want to use it to steer her away from him."

"How's that going to work?" she asks.

I shrug. "Post misleading love advice and get Kamryn to read it."

Hannah regards me suspiciously. "What's it to you who Kamryn likes?"

Ah. This is where it gets tricky. I don't want to tell my best friend that I'm crushing hard on the most popular girl in our grade. I'm afraid she'll tell me I don't stand a chance with Kamryn. Or worse, she'll laugh. Hannah's not one to keep her opinions to herself.

I shrug again. "It's more about not letting Kyle have the satisfaction of yet another girl wasting her love on him."

Hannah peels the sticker off the apple and flattens it on the counter. "You should let Kyle have her," she says. "They'd be perfect for each other."

"What do you mean?"

Hannah shrugs.

"What?" I ask again.

But she doesn't say anything else.

I say, "I think my idea could work. Plus it would be fun to get the school hooked on a relationship blog."

"But it's bogus!" Hannah protests.

I shake my head. "Only the Kamryn-Kyle posts," I say. "The rest of it can be legit. Real advice."

Hannah sighs. "What if you put all that energy into skating instead, Owen? Or helping me organize the Free the Children Gala?"

"Come on," I say. "How much fun would it be to mess with a thousand people's heads like this?"

Her eyes get a faraway look.

Good. She's thinking about it.

When she looks back at me, I raise an eyebrow. I move in for the kill. Playing on her do-gooder side. "Think of all the lives you'd be touching," I say. "You could really help people…find love and all that."

She tilts her head. "It *would* be kind of fun to see the response it gets."

"So you're in?"

"I'm not saying I'll *write* anything."

"So you're in?" I repeat, giving her leg a little nudge with my foot.

"You could get in big trouble if this ever gets out, Owen."

"It won't. I'll make sure of it."

Hannah looks up at the ceiling and releases a long, slow breath. When she looks back at me, there's a gleam in her eye.

"I'm in."

Chapter Five

I lean back in my chair. "What number are we up to?"

It's Sunday afternoon. Hannah's on my bed with her laptop open. She studies the sheet where we keep track of user names and passwords. The "phantom people" who write to the Oracle for advice.

"Seventeen. Both questions and answers." She consults the sheet. "We've got the messy breakup, the cheating girlfriend, the jealous lover, the gay who's afraid to come out, the hopeless romantic, the fetishist—"

"I liked that one. Sneaker Sniffer." I stretch. "Let's do one about Kamryn and Kyle now."

"Ugh." Hannah rolls her eyes. "Fine." She starts typing, setting up a new phantom email for the question writer. "Number eighteen," she says. "I'll call her QB."

"Quintessential babe?"

Hannah stares. "You think Kamryn's a babe?" Her laugh is short. "Holy, you're just like everyone else."

I realize my mistake. "Well, I myself don't think she's a babe," I scramble. "I mean, not *personally*."

Hannah looks back down at her laptop. "Whatever. QB stands for Queen Bee."

She looks mad. I'm not sure what to say. Usually if Hannah's mad about something, you hear about it.

But she doesn't say anything else.

I keep us moving along.

"Okay, so. Our question for Kamryn could be, *How do I get this really hot guy to notice me?*"

Hannah starts typing. A few seconds later, she hits a button. "Sent," she says.

I click *Refresh* on my laptop, and the question appears on my screen as though QB actually wrote in to ask the Oracle about it.

I grab my head and groan.

"What?" Hannah asks.

"Epic problem," I say.

"What?" she asks again.

"I want to give her the wrong advice and steer her in the wrong direction," I say. "But the Oracle isn't supposed to give bad advice. It's supposed to give *good* advice."

"Oh," Hannah says. "Riiiiiight."

We sit for a few moments.

Then Hannah snaps her fingers. "Got it," she says.

"What?"

"We write in as Kyle."

I stare at her. "We write in as Kyle?" I can't imagine my brother reading a website about relationships, let alone writing in to ask for advice. But Kamryn won't know that.

"What would Kyle ask?" I say.

"*Dear Oracle*," Hannah begins. She types as she talks.

"*I'm in grade ten. There's this grade-eight girl who's driving me crazy. She has a crush on me, but the feeling isn't mutual. She's on the prowl and won't let up. She's even got plans to hunt me down at the spring dance.*"

My jaw drops, and I swivel in my chair. "That's so obvious!"

Hannah looks at me. "Owen. Do you want her to figure it out or what?"

"Right. Obvious it is."

She finishes. *"Oracle, I'm not interested in dating little kids. How do I tell her to leave me alone?"*

I can't help it. I laugh. "That's perfect! If Kamryn reads that question, she'll totally think Kyle wrote it. She'll get the message loud and clear." I lean back and punch Hannah on the shoulder. "You're a genius."

"I know." She shrugs and twirls a length of hair around a finger. "Your world would be dead and meaningless without me."

I laugh again. "You realize, don't you, that if people start reading this website, we can totally direct their behavior with questions and answers?"

Hannah nods. "Supreme power."

"That's pretty cool. To have this much control over people."

"Controlling minds is pretty cool," she agrees. "Except there's one tiny problem."

"What's that?"

"How do we get people to read it?"

"You do the main floor. I'll do upstairs." I hand Hannah a fistful of blue business cards.

She heads down the corridor, slipping a card into every few lockers. The hallways are quiet except for the mad-science nerds and a few people in the drama club. Almost everyone has gone home or to the gym to watch the game.

Hannah and I stayed up late last night creating anonymous identities. Inventing questions and posting answers and having way too much fun.

As of today, the Oracle is open for business.

I take my bundle of cards upstairs. Between us, we have three hundred. It's not enough for every locker at

LaMontagne, but it's a good start for getting the word out.

I glance down at the card. It shows a dark sky full of stars swirling around an image of an ancient temple. In gold are the words, *Is love in the stars for you at LaMontagne? Ask the Oracle.* The URL is at the bottom.

It should get people's attention.

I save the last card for Kamryn's locker, at the far end of the east wing. If nothing else, I have to make sure she gets one. She's the whole reason for the Oracle.

As I drop the card through a small opening at the top of the locker, it hits me that I should have written a personal message on it. An invitation, or maybe a hint about Kyle. Something to make sure she logs on and checks out the site. I duck my head to feel around at the bottom of the locker, but there's no way I'm retrieving the card.

That was dumb.

I pull on the locker. Locked, of course. I bang my forehead against it in frustration.

Hannah rounds the corner. "This is going to be so great!" she says. She stops short when she sees me. "What on earth are you doing?"

I straighten guiltily. "Nothing."

"Why were you smashing your head against…" Hannah pulls back and scans the row of lockers. "Kamryn's locker?" she finishes. When she looks back at me, her eyes are suspicious. A locker slams in the next hallway.

"Oh, is this her locker?" I feign surprise. "That's weird. I, uh, didn't have enough cards to get to the end of this row. I was just thinking that maybe we didn't print enough."

I can tell she doesn't believe me.

She opens her mouth to speak.

Mason rounds the corner, wearing those jumbo foam hands people wave at hockey games. He stops and points, cowboy-style, when he sees us. "Dudes," he says. "What're you doing up here? Game's in the gym."

Hannah looks at Mason, then at me.

"We were just headed there," she says. "Let's go."

Chapter Six

The next day after school, I check the Oracle's stats.

If I wasn't sitting down already, I would have fallen on the floor. The site had two hundred and twenty-three hits and forty-eight comments.

My stomach does a flip-flop.

What?

My heart hammers. I should be happy, but instead I feel like I've been buried by an avalanche.

What have I started?

What am I going to do with forty-eight questions? How will I answer them all?

I run my hands through my hair, then click on the first one.

Dear Oracle. My best friend just broke up with her boyfriend. I'm really attracted to him and want to go out with him, But I don't want my friend to be upset. What do I do? —LF

I blink. Wow, that's a tough one.

Maybe the next question will be easier to answer. I click on it.

Dear Oracle. Is it a good idea to kiss on the first date? My friends and I can't agree. —To Kiss or Not to Kiss

I don't know. *Is* it a good idea?

Let's have a look at number three.

Dear Oracle. I'm going out with a guy that I'm not interested in anymore.

How do I dump him gently? —Softhearted

Ah, man. Who was I to think I could manage a gig like this?

I go through every question to see if any of them are easy to answer.

None are, except for the one asking about poisoning an ex's new girlfriend with formaldehyde from the chem lab. I write a stern reply discouraging the idea. Before I hit *Send* I suggest itching powder in her gym shorts instead.

I drop my head into my hands. I've told everyone the Oracle can solve their trickiest relationship issues. And, other than telling people not to kill each other, I don't have a clue where to start.

The doorbell rings, making me jump.

"Forty-eight questions!" Hannah says when I open the door. She's obviously checked the stats too.

"I know," I groan. "I have no idea how to answer them either."

Hannah grins. "I do."

"What? How?"

"Horoscopes."

"Horoscopes?"

She nods. "Astrology. You ask people to send in the birthdate of the person they're asking about. It's the best tool we have to tailor the Oracle's advice to that person."

"I'm not following you."

Hannah steps inside and closes the door.

"You're a Sagittarius, right?" she asks.

"I don't know. Am I?"

"Yes, you are. Your birthday is December eighth." She starts walking toward my bedroom.

I follow her. "Okay. So what?"

"Well, according to the ancient art of astrology, there are certain things a person can do if he or she wants to woo someone of a particular sign."

"Keep talking."

"Well, let's use you as an example," she says, settling herself on my bed. "Sagittarians are honest, and they have a great sense of humor. So good relationship advice for someone who's in love with a Sagittarius is to show that you can be a lot of fun. Or that you like the outdoors. Or horses."

I look at Hannah. "How'd you get so wise on astrology all of a sudden?"

Hannah pulls out a folded sheet of paper and waves it at me. "Google." She opens the sheet and runs her finger down a list, reading. "More on Sagittarius. Optimistic. Adventurous. You like to travel. You think about the future. You don't like to be tied down."

I laugh and sit down. "No comment. What's your sign?"

"I'm a Leo," she says.

"What's that mean?"

She raises an eyebrow. "Flatter me."

"Anything else?"

"That's all you need to know for Leos," says Hannah.

"Okay, so…you're brilliant," I say.

"Tell me something I don't know."

"You have lovely, uh…hair?"

"Getting warmer." She laughs. I love making Hannah laugh. Her laugh makes me feel good.

"You have a laugh that I could listen to all day?" I say.

Hannah stops laughing. She blinks, twice, then looks down.

The air in the room feels different all of a sudden. The tops of my ears grow hot.

I hear Hannah take in a little breath. Then she nods toward the laptop. "We should get started. We need to get the word out so people can write in with actual birthdates."

"Right." I nod. "But wait. How are people supposed to know other people's birthdates? You can't go up to a girl or guy you like and ask them what their birthday is. That's too obvious. They'd know you were writing a question for the Oracle."

Hannah leans over my shoulder. She smells good. Like vanilla. And fruit.

With a couple of clicks, she brings up a familiar blue page.

"Facebook, silly."

The girl is brilliant. Of course! Everyone puts their birthday on their page.

"Awesome! You are *so* smart!"

She shrugs and studies her nails modestly. "I try."

I open up a new post and start typing.

Dear Readers. I am truly delighted that so many of you have written in with your questions. As I see it, to receive the most accurate advice possible, please include the birthdate of the individual in question.

"That's going to cause problems," Hannah says, looking over my shoulder.

"I thought you said that was the best way to do it?" I say. "If we have the people's birthdates, we can tailor the advice better, right?"

"But if they write the birthdate right into their comment," Hannah says, "everyone who reads it can figure out who they're talking about."

"Ohhh," I say. "Hadn't thought of that. Well. What if they post the question in the comments, and then send it to us again in an email? With the birthdate included?"

Hannah's eyes brighten. "Email's private. That would totally work."

I add, *Of course, you won't want to put the birthdate in your comment. Unless you want your secret longings to become public! Post your comment, then send it to me again in an email at oracle98@gmail.com. Be sure to include your would-be's birthdate.*

"Good?" I ask.

"Excellent," she answers.

I click *Publish*.

"Now for today's questions," Hannah says.

I roll my eyes. "Ugh. There's forty-eight!" I say.

Hannah glances back at the screen. "Fifty-six, actually. Look."

I don't look. "That's way too many to answer," I moan.

"Who says we have to answer all of them?" Hannah asks. "It's not like people are paying for this. They can wait their turn. Actually, a wait might stoke the fires." She gives me a half smile.

"I'm not so sure I can handle this fire getting stoked any higher," I say.

That came out weird. I feel my ears start to burn again. Hannah's face goes pink.

Her next words save me from putting my foot any farther into my mouth. "Why don't we just pick the five best and answer those?"

I stare at her. The five best. It's perfect. I want to hug her.

But I don't.

I nod. "Okay. Five. We can do five. Where do we start?"

Chapter Seven

At school, everyone is talking about the Oracle. I catch snippets of conversation all through the day.

"Did you read the one from SS?"

"That the shoe chick?"

"Yeah, Sneaker Sniffer."

"I wonder who that could be? Weird thing to get off on."

I resist the urge to smile.

People are still talking about the site when I head to math help after school.

I'm helping a guy in grade seven apply the order of operations when a bag skids onto the table beside me. A book slaps down on the tabletop, then a phone, then a pencil. And finally, Kamryn flops into the chair across from me with a dramatic sigh. Two grade-seven girls at a nearby table stare as the goddess makes her entrance.

My heart does a complete somersault before coming back to rest in the center of my body. "Hi," I say, before I can decide against it.

"This is stupid," she says. Her eyes move around the room.

"Actually, it's math help," I say. The grade-seven kid chuckles.

Kamryn narrows her eyes and lets them rest on me. I force myself to meet her gaze. It's green. And cold.

My love is like to ice and I to fire.

"I mean, *being* here is stupid," she says. "It's a waste of time."

I can't help it. My natural habit of arguing—honed from years of living with a jerk brother—surfaces. "Door's over there." I nod toward it.

I want to kick myself as soon as the words hit the air. How long have I wanted to get Kamryn in my orbit? And now that I have her sitting across from me, I suggest that she leave?

"I can't leave," she growls. "Stupid old Saddlebags won't let me. She said I had to come. Otherwise I fail this semester."

I steal a glance toward Ms. Hamilton's desk, hoping she didn't overhear. But she's not even in the room. "Saddlebags?"

Kamryn fixes me with a withering glare. "Yeah, Saddlebags. That would be our fat, ugly math teacher with the huge butt that drips down the sides of her legs."

I'd laugh at Kamryn's words if her delivery weren't so mean. The grade-seven

53

kid beside me laughs again. Kamryn looks away, mad that her sarcasm is wasted on a couple of nerds.

"Listen," she says and looks right at me. "Can you just show me how to do this? Then I can get out of here." She flips open her binder and pulls out a sheet of paper. A pop quiz. Zero out of six. She slides the paper across the table at me and taps it with her pencil. Twice. *Tap tap*.

I look at the pencil. At the nicely shaped nails attached to the fingers that are holding the pencil. And I look up, at Kamryn's face. Her stunning, beautiful, flawless face. She's not looking at me anymore. She's looking at the clock over my head.

Ice.

"Sure," I say. "Just let me finish this problem with Matteo."

Kamryn's eyes slide back to my face. She looks confused. "Can't you do it now?" She wiggles the paper a bit. "Come on,

I've got to be somewhere." She dips her chin a bit and raises one eyebrow, coaxing me. "Please?" She blinks twice and smiles. "You owe me anyway, from last week. At the 7-Eleven."

I look at her. My tongue ties itself up in a knot. A hundred thoughts crowd my brain. That she's perfect. That she shouldn't try to butt in front of other people, because it's not fair. That my shirt still bears the stains from her Coke Slurpee.

But, of course, I don't tell her any of those things.

Matteo solves the problem for me. He's a pretty cool kid, and he's obviously not scared of Kamryn.

"Owen's helping me right now," Matteo says. "You'll have to wait your turn."

The girls at the next table send up a muted gasp at his daring. Who in their right mind sasses Kamryn Holt?

Kamryn's face folds in and pinches up. Her lips thin as she turns to Matteo. "I'm sorry. Were you talking to me?"

"I was, yes." Matteo nods. His voice is thin and nasal. He meets her gaze straight on. "I said that Owen's almost finished showing me how these brackets work. Then I'm sure he'd be delighted to help you. Wouldn't you, Owen?"

He's absolutely right. But still, I feel caught.

I don't answer.

Kamryn stares at Matteo for a few seconds. He stares right back. The room is silent as a snowdrift as she makes up her mind whether she's going to admit defeat or escalate the drama.

She chooses both.

In one angry movement, her hand flashes forward. She snatches the paper Matteo and I have been using and crumples it. With a dismissive little hiss, she drops the wadded-up paper on the table.

She pushes her chair back from the table. "I don't *wait*," she says. She looks around the room. "I don't need to practice math with a bunch of *retards* either."

At the word *retard*, my anger flares. I have an autistic cousin. But even if I didn't, I still hate people using that word as a put-down. Doesn't matter how perfect they are.

Kamryn slings her bag over her shoulder. She gathers up her book and phone and flounces from the room. She slams the door hard enough to shake the windows in their panes.

The girls let out a collective breath. Matteo picks up his crumpled paper. My mouth, which had opened to say something about the retard comment, snaps shut.

"Wow, Matteo, you really made her mad," says one of the girls.

"That was *awesome*!" whispers the other.

"She's a cow," Matteo says. "I don't know why people let her get away with it." He carefully flattens his paper against the tabletop and scoots his chair closer. He appears entirely unfazed by the whole interaction. The girls are eyeing him with a new appreciation.

"So, yeah, anyway," he says to me, holding his pencil over his paper. "Do you mind showing me again? From the beginning?"

Chapter Eight

By the following week, Hannah and I have upped our allotment to fifteen questions a day. People are going nuts over the Oracle.

The routine goes like this. I read Hannah the questions. Most days, there are between ten and twenty. We choose which ones to answer based on how much information we have. Hannah does the horoscope research, and I compile the answers. All told, it's about an hour's work.

Today we get our first feedback.

"Listen to this," I say.

"Listening." Hannah is stretched out on my bed watching a Leo forecast on YouTube.

"No, you're not."

She sighs and presses *Pause*. "Okay. I am now."

I read, "*Dear Oracle. That girl I wanted to ask out last week? I took your advice and used little cut-up bits of magazines to spell out the words to ask her out on a date. I said, 'Want to go check out the art gallery?' and then I gave it to her at the end of break. And you know what? She loved it. She said she didn't know any other guy who would take her to a gallery on a first date. Thanks!*"

"Aw, that is so sweet," Hannah says. "Owen, you're a matchmaker now!" She pats my back.

"It's not me," I say. "It's the horoscopes. And you," I add, with a half shrug.

Hannah blushes. "Read me today's questions."

"Well, I've already drafted a response to this one," I say. "This one's kind of heavy." I glance at her. "There's some messed-up kids out there."

Her brow furrows. "Read it."

"It's from someone called Losing Hope," I begin. "*Dear Oracle. I can't take it anymore. Last night my dad got really angry with me. Again. He was drinking. He was mad because I didn't have enough money to go buy him cigarettes.*"

Hannah sits up. "What?"

I keep reading.

"*So he broke all the dishes, one by one. And then he made me clean up the mess. With my hands.*"

"*What?*" Hannah whispers.

I finish the note. "*I don't know what to do. If I run away, I'll end up living on the streets. I'm seriously thinking about just ending it all. Maybe I can start over in another lifetime.*"

I turn to Hannah. "Signed, *Losing Hope.*"

Hannah swallows. "Someone actually had that happen to them?"

I nod slowly. "Someone at our school."

"Who?" she asks. Her question hangs in the air, heavy and sad.

I shake my head. "Who knows?"

"What did you tell her?" Hannah's voice quavers.

"Kids' Help Phone," I say. "As a first step. I also googled *teen depression domestic violence* and came up with a number for the National Domestic Violence Hotline."

Hannah shudders. She stares down at her hands. I know she, like me, will spend tomorrow looking for people with cuts on their hands.

"And," I add, "I said she had to tell someone at school—a trusted adult. Maybe a teacher or the counselor. I said there's people who can help, and there are safe places to go."

Hannah nods. "I hope she's okay," she whispers. She looks out my window.

"I hope so too," I say. And I really do. I think about how kids like that don't often report abuse because they don't want their parents to get in trouble. So they take it. Until they can't take it anymore.

I don't want *Losing Hope* to be like that. I'll check in with her again sometime soon. See how she's doing. Whether she's reached out to someone yet.

I glance back at Hannah. "Do you need to take a break?" I ask.

She takes a deep breath and shakes her head. "No, we can go on." She pauses.

"I think you did a good job on that one. There's not much else you can do right now."

I shrug. "I wish I could do more."

"Let's keep an eye out for when *Losing Hope* surfaces again," she says. "I hope she does."

I nod. "Me too."

Chapter Nine

"Keep reading," Hannah says.

I read a dozen questions out loud. When I get to the last one, my heart skips a beat. Skips about eleven beats, actually. Maybe twelve.

It's signed *Heart Huntress*.

I take in a long breath. "Whoooee," I say. "Here we go."

"What?"

"Kamryn has finally written in."

Instantly, Hannah appears behind me. She reads aloud over my shoulder. "*Dear Oracle. The guy I want is older than me by a couple of grades, but I know we'd be perfect together. He's already noticed me, and I think he likes what he sees. Here's my question. I'm going to see him again at the dance this week, and I want that to be the night I capture his heart. I need your advice, from how to make my grand entrance until the moment I nail that first kiss.*"

"Huh," I say. "She didn't understand that message we wrote as Kyle. Or she didn't realize it was directed at her."

"I'm not surprised," Hannah says.

"What do you mean?"

"Honestly, Owen," Hannah says. She sounds exasperated. "Kamryn thinks she's above it all. If everyone else thinks she's perfect, why wouldn't she? She has no reason to imagine that she can't get exactly what she wants.

It would never occur to her that the post was written by Kyle."

"It wasn't," I point out.

Hannah groans. "You know what I mean!"

I grin and open my Gmail. "Anyway, we need to redirect her. Tell her to do all the wrong things so she turns Kyle off."

"Heavy perfume," Hannah offers. "Lots of makeup. Thick, heavy lipstick, especially."

I recoil in mock horror. "Gross!"

"Well?" Hannah asks. "You want ways to turn guys off, don't you?"

I check for Kamryn's message that contains the birthdate of the guy in question. Sure enough, she's copied the same message but added *Birthday October 30th.*

"October thirtieth," I say. "That's Kyle."

"Ooh, he's a Scorpio," says Hannah. "Sexiest sign in the zodiac." Her voice is teasing.

"You can't be serious." I can't even think about it. Kyle? Sexy? The guy gets those silverfish bugs in his toothbrush because it's so dirty.

"But Scorpios can be really mean," she adds.

"That's more like it."

"I don't know why you want to mess with karma on this one." Hannah sighs. "Kyle's a perfect fit for Kamryn. Mean deserves mean."

I roll my eyes. "Oh my god," I say. "She's not *that* bad. You've got some weird vendetta against Kamryn."

"Um, excuse me?" Hannah says. "You were the one who told me how she shot Matteo down in flames during your tutorial."

I shrug. "Maybe she was having a bad day."

"Oh right. That day, *and* the time at 7-Eleven? Come on, Owen. I know what she's like."

"Why do you always have to come down so hard on her?" I ask.

"Why are you so eager to excuse her crappy behavior?" Hannah shoots back. "Wait, no, I know. Because you're *in love*." She holds both hands over her heart and flutters her eyelashes.

Normally, I'd laugh off her teasing. But sudden hot anger spills into my throat. I'm mad that she thinks I'm an idiot for liking Kamryn.

But I'm also mad at myself, because a little part of me knows she's right.

I say the first thing I can think of that will hurt. "You're right, Hannah. I *am* in love with Kamryn."

Hannah goes very still.

I drive the knife in a little deeper. "And that makes you crazy, doesn't it? Maybe you're jealous."

She flinches. Immediately, I regret my words. I open my mouth, searching for a way to take them back.

"Hannah," I say.

But it's too late. I watch, helpless, as she gathers her laptop and bag.

"Hannah, listen."

The handle makes a soft *click* as the door closes behind her.

I stare at the screen for a long time after she's gone. What did I say all that for? I've embarrassed Hannah and made her feel terrible.

Holy. Who's the mean one now?

A new comment drops in as I'm sitting there. It jolts me out of my trance.

I'm on my own now. Guess I'd better get going.

I ignore the new question and start with Kamryn's instead. A few minutes ago, I was excited. Finally! My long-awaited chance to steer Kamryn away from Kyle!

But my fingers feel frozen as I type my reply.

Dear Huntress. As I see it, your would-be is already in love with another young woman. But the stars show me that the universe is unfolding as it should.

Those words seem familiar. They just kind of typed themselves out onto the page. I wonder where I've heard those before? Maybe in a poem.

I shrug and continue.

While you may believe deeply in your wish to be united with this guy, my observations show me a more powerful match in a young man closer to your age. The clouds obscure my sight from complete clarity, but I sense that this individual is—

Is what? In grade eight? Wears jeans and zombie T-shirts? That's a bit too clear.

I think about where Kamryn and I cross paths. The only place I can think of where we've actually exchanged words and glances—besides outside the convenience store—is in math help.

I go back to my reply. *I sense that this individual is logical in nature. I see you meeting him outside class time, perhaps in an extracurricular session. He is helping you with something. There is some numeric energy there, but I can't quite pinpoint it.*

I wonder if this is too tea-leafy. Or whether the numeric bit is too obvious. But what do I have to lose?

Try exploring that avenue. Good luck.

I take a deep breath and hit *Publish*.

I turn my attention to the list of waiting questions. Methodically, I work my way through them, check traits against zodiac signs and design my advice to suit. I don't rush any of them. I even throw in a bit of my own advice when I think it'll be helpful.

In between questions, I think about my response to Kamryn. I wonder if it's going to work.

I sigh. Whatever. It's out there now. Time will tell where it leads.

I should be excited at nailing that long-awaited interaction with her. Or nervous, at least.

But all I can think of are my last words to Hannah. And the look on her face as I said them.

Chapter Ten

Kamryn must have read the Oracle, because she is at math help today. She hangs out for almost half an hour at my table. Never mind that it feels awkward and we have nothing to talk about. That's to be expected at the start of a relationship. Right?

We do a little math too. So there.

I walk home like I'm on a cloud.

After I fix myself a snack, I head up to my room to check the blog. I'm surprised to already find an entry from Heart Huntress.

Dear Oracle. I went looking for that number-logical guy today. The helper? I'm not sure if I was looking in the right place. The guy I sat with was nice enough, but we didn't really have anything in common, and I didn't exactly feel a spark. I think I might have got the wrong guy. —HH

Nothing in common?

No spark?

I chew my lip for a couple of minutes. How can I make her feel a spark?

I force myself to read through a few other questions before I write her back. I need to think through my reply.

The questions people write in with keep getting better and better. A couple of people have written in seeking advice about their friendships. One guy asked me to help him talk his sister out of getting a tattoo of her boyfriend's name on her arm. Another asked me where he could find cool shirts cheap. I don't feel like a fraud when I'm advising people on stuff like where to buy clothes or how to handle their parents' embarrassing social habits.

Only when I'm deliberately misleading people in love.

I pick the questions I'll answer today. I tell one girl that her brother's friend has no right to pressure her to give him pictures of herself in a bikini. I tell another that since this is the third time she's caught her boyfriend in a big lie, it's time to cut him loose, even though it'll hurt. I explain to one guy that if his current flame doesn't respond to his texts within a day, then yeah, she's losing the love.

Only after I'm finished these do I allow myself to settle into a response to Kamryn.

Dear Huntress. As I see it—

I like that part, that "as I see it" bit. Makes the advice sound sort of fortune-telly.

As I see it, you absolutely had the correct person today.

Wow, it feels so…so…*out there* to write that.

But there aren't exactly a lot of options. If I'm going to use the Oracle to steer Kamryn into my world, I've got to be crazy and direct.

I decide I'm okay with it.

But I need something to get us further down this road I've started us on.

I need a ruse. Something to get us talking.

Today Mr. Winehouse mentioned we'll be starting our research projects on early civilizations in social studies.

It's the perfect setup.

I see an opportunity to work with this young man in a partnership. You will be reading, or writing, or creating media. It will be about something ancient, but I can't see exactly what.

I decide to leave her with some very specific instructions.

You will need to approach him. If you don't, he will choose a different partner.

Then, for the clincher, I add, *And the course of your life will be forever changed.*

And then I click *Publish*.

On Monday, everybody's talking about the dance. I had to stay home with my mom, who'd just had a wisdom tooth pulled and was still loopy from the painkillers.

Kyle sure wasn't going to miss it.

So I stayed home.

It *sounded* like it was fun. Kyle brought home some other girl, not Kamryn. They stayed up late watching

Invasion of the Body Snatchers, and then I didn't see him for the rest of the weekend.

So Kamryn is, without a doubt, not on Kyle's radar.

A greedy little part of me rubs its hands at the thought, She's *mine*, all mine. The rational side of me shrieks with terror—what am I going to *do* if she takes the Oracle seriously and decides to come after me?

I find out soon enough. In third period, Mr. Winehouse tells us about our research projects. Ancient civilizations.

"This project requires partner work, people," says Mr. Winehouse now. "Two heads are better than one."

As soon as the words leave his mouth, there's the familiar rustle as people turn in their seats to make eye contact. I keep my head down. I focus intently on the Dementor I'm doodling in the side of my page. I hope Morgan doesn't ask me to work with him. Normally, I'd be happy to, but today…

A hand taps my shoulder, and I jump, jabbing a thick line of ink through my Dementor's hood.

I turn. Kamryn is standing beside my desk. She looks kind of mad.

"What's that?" Her eyes are on the Dementor. It's pretty good, I think. He's floating in midair, and his cloak is in tatters. It wisps out behind him as he slides along.

"It's a Dementor," I say.

She pulls her brows together a bit. "A mental what?" she says.

"A *Dementor*," I say. "From *Harry Potter*?"

"Oh." She tosses her head, sounding bored. "So listen, do you have a partner?"

"Not yet," I say.

She looks away. "Do you want to do the Romans or the Mayans?"

What if I wanted to do the Mesopotamians? Wait. Did she even ask me if I wanted to be her partner? My mind fumbles for protocol.

"Whichever," I say. "I'm easy."

"Let's do the Mayans," she says, sitting in the desk behind me. She pulls out her iPad and sets it on the tabletop. "Tuesdays and Thursdays are the only days I can meet after school, so we need to get a lot done during class."

I nod. "Okay." I want to ask her how the dance went, but I can't for the life of me figure out how to bring it up.

I already know enough though. Things didn't work out with her and Kyle.

She pushes the iPad toward me. "Look at the outline," she says, pointing to the black screen. "Wino said it's on the class web page. We want to make sure we get everything in there."

"Wino?" The second the words are out of my mouth, I realize she's talking about Mr. Winehouse.

She rolls her eyes.

"Never mind," I say. "I get it." I'm irritated that I asked.

I touch the screen and bring up our class page.

Kamryn looks around the room, bored, while I locate our assignment. On *her* iPad. While she just sits there.

She squints at me. "Do you read the Oracle?" Her question is sudden.

My ears grow hot. I am so glad my hair covers them.

"Nope," I say, without looking up. "What's that?"

"Nothing," she says. "Just some website."

Then she sits forward and looks me up and down. She scrunches her eyes up a little bit. "Do you always wear skater clothes? Or do you ever wear, I don't know, nice stuff?"

I'm shocked that she put me down like that, right to my face. She's kind of fearless.

I'm kind of embarrassed.

And now I'm pissed off.

I speak before I think. Force of habit.

"Do you ever say nice things?" I ask. "Or do you only, I don't know, say mean stuff?"

Kamryn stares at me for a couple of seconds, then sits back in her chair. She folds her arms.

"Just hurry up and find the assignment," she says, jerking her chin toward the iPad. "Let's get this over with."

Chapter Eleven

On Tuesday afternoon, Kamryn and I head to my place. Today we'll finish off our research on Mayan religious systems and start our Museum Box online. I hope this will be less strained than yesterday's in-class session. We talked so little, I think we managed to blow through nearly all of our research.

Awkward.

"This is nice," Kamryn says as she steps into my house. Her eyes move around the room approvingly. "Your parents have great design sense."

"My mom stages homes for realtors," I say. "She can make a rodent hole look like the Waldorf Astoria."

Kamryn's eyes drift to the trophy on the bookcase. There's only one on display at any time, even though there are more than twelve tucked away in various closets. Pretty soon we'll need to build a shed to house all of Kyle's achievements.

"Who's the basketball star?"

"That'd be my brother."

Her eyes cut to me. "I didn't know you had a brother."

I shrug. That would be because I intentionally didn't tell you, I think.

"How old is he?"

"Sixteen." I kick off my shoes and head down the hallway toward my bedroom. Kamryn follows. The door to Kyle's room is closed.

"Where does he go to school?"

"LaMontagne. Senior campus." For whatever reason, our school is split into two separate buildings—the middle grades and the senior high. It's a relief not to have to share space with Kyle all day. I get enough of that every evening.

"What's his name?"

I sigh. "Kyle."

Here it comes.

"Kyle…*Roberts*?" The word comes out as a shriek.

"Same one."

Kamryn's hands fly up to cover her mouth. "Oh my god, I had no idea he was your *brother*!" She looks like a kid who's just spotted Santa Claus filling her stocking with diamonds and PEZ.

I shrug. "Well. Owen Roberts. Kyle Roberts. You know."

"Yeah, but, I…you don't. I mean, you don't look…like him at all, you know?"

"Thanks," I say.

"No, I mean…" Kamryn flaps her hands. She looks around, as though Kyle might appear from behind a secret door. "Is he home?"

Why did I bother? What good did I think it would do to use the Oracle to try to force Kamryn to like me?

"No."

"Oh." She looks disappointed.

Thankfully, her questions dry up once we enter my room. While she drifts around looking at the sketches on my wall, I open up my laptop. I pop up a new tab and google *Mayan religious customs*.

"I didn't know you were an artist," Kamryn says, moving from one picture to the next. "These are really good."

"Thanks," I say. A little flicker of hope lights in my belly, and I turn my chair to face her.

"Does Kyle draw?"

I rotate back to the computer.

"Nope."

"What does he do? Like, hobby-wise?"

What was I thinking, anyway? You can't force someone to like you. Even I know that. Making Kamryn do this project with me seems pathetic now.

I glance at the clock in the corner of the screen. I'd rather be out at the skate park, blowing off steam. Like Kamryn said yesterday, let's get this over with.

"Look, Kamryn," I say. "I have to be somewhere at four. So we should get going."

She looks disappointed. I guess she wanted to talk about Kyle some more. "Okay." She unzips her backpack and slides out her iPad. "Have you got anything to eat?"

I'm embarrassed that I haven't offered. Even rude guests deserve to be offered refreshments. "Of course," I say. "I'll go grab something."

I push back from my desk and hurry to the kitchen. Now that I think about it, I'm starving.

I take bread and cheese out of the fridge and turn the oven on to *broil*. I flip on the kitchen sound system. The room fills with Calm Radio piano solos. My mom's favorite.

I change it to skate punk.

I sigh. Now that Kamryn knows I'm Kyle's brother, chances are she's going to want to hang around with me more to be closer to him.

That should be a good thing, right? That we spend more time together? Except.

She'll be doing it because of him, not because of me.

And Hannah's right. She's not very nice.

Even Kamryn was right. We have almost nothing in common.

Plus, Kamryn has zero sense of humor.

I swipe a knife out of the block and shave off thin slices of cheddar. I pile them on two slices of bread. I slide the tray into the oven and grab an apple. I polish it on my jeans, like I've seen Hannah do.

Hannah.

I've lost touch with one of my best friends while getting myself tangled up in a web of dishonesty with someone I'm not sure I want anymore.

Stupid.

I wash and slice the apple.

When I open the oven door a few minutes later, the cheese toast is bubbling. Perfect. I slide the pan out onto the stovetop to cool, and then I grab plates.

Then I remember.

I didn't lock the screen on my computer before I left my room.

Oh crap.

My stomach plummets.

I throw the plates on the counter and pound down the hallway back to my room, my heart slamming.

I skid to a stop at my doorway. My eyes wheel around the room in panic. "Kamryn?"

She's not here.

"Kamryn?" I yell.

No answer.

Her bag's gone.

She left. The music must have been too loud for me to hear her leave.

Crap.

I bolt toward my computer and slide onto the chair. The wheels roll me sideways, smashing my knees against my bookcase.

I paw at the trackpad to get rid of the screensaver.

When the screen fills, I'm not looking at a website on Mayan religious customs. Not at all.

I'm looking at the Oracle.

She found it.

And she wrote about it. In a post. And her post is on the home page, which means she published it too.

The title screams at me. *The Oracle is A LIE!*

I skim the post.

There it is. Plain as day. Out there in the ether for everyone to see.

Listen up, people! This isn't the Oracle writing to you. This is another student at LaMontagne. The Oracle is all made up.

I feel like puking.

I've just discovered that Owen Roberts writes the posts. "As I see it," (ha ha), you have been telling your secrets to a grade-eight idiot loser... and he's been making up answers to try and trick you!

I bite down on the irony. I wasn't trying to trick anyone except Kamryn. For everyone else, I did my absolute best to advise them wisely. And now she's calling me out as a cheat.

But how do I prove otherwise? I can't argue with her.

There's no fixing this.

This is going to be the end of my days at school.

Chapter Twelve

I don't want to get out of bed the next day. How do I face a world that thinks my blog is a sham? That *I'm* a sham?

The thing is, it doesn't feel like a sham at all. I was proud of the Oracle. I liked helping people. Or what I thought was helping people.

I heave my legs over the side of the bed and sit up. I rub my face.

Today is the first day of the rest of my life at LaMontagne. And is it ever going to look different from this point forward.

At school, I keep my head down and my feet moving. A lot of people stare at me. People in Kamryn's posse whisper hissy comments to each other while glaring in my direction.

I want to talk to Hannah, but I've bungled that friendship beyond repair. She's not coming back.

There is a lot of whispering. But no one talks to me.

No one, that is, except Mason.

He catches up with me on the way to Spanish. "Hey, man," he says. "Don't sweat it. It'll pass. I love the Oracle. Everybody loves the Oracle."

"You think?" I ask.

He nods. "For sure! It's great reading." He claps me on the shoulder, then drops his voice. "But I have to ask you, little man. What possessed you to set up a relationship blog?"

I smile at my nickname. Mason is four inches shorter than me.

"You really want to know?" I ask.

"I really want to know."

I look around to make sure we're not overheard. Not like I have anything to hide now. "Did you read the posts by Heart Huntress?"

Mason nods again.

"That was Kamryn Holt. I set up the blog as a way to kill her crush on my brother. Try to get her to go out with me instead."

Mason looks thoughtful for a moment. That's rare, so I appreciate it when it happens. He glances toward Kamryn and Dana, who are spitting evil looks at me.

He looks back at me. "D'it work?"

I shake my head. "Not a chance. Killed my crush on *her* though."

He grins. "Probably worth it, then." He looks back at Kamryn and lowers his voice. "I could've told you you're wasting your time, man."

He's not the only one.

On our way to assembly on Friday, Jon and Ryan catch up to us in the hallway.

"Hey, man," says Jon.

I look over. "Hey."

Jon and I don't hang out, but I've known him since grade school. He's a good guy.

"So, uh, I was Rubber Duckie."

I smile. "No way. Really?" Right away I want to know how his conversation went with the girl on his swim team. "How'd it go? Did you manage to get her alone, without all of her friends around?"

He grins. "Yeah. I asked Coach to tell her to help me roll up the lane ropes." He laughs. "It was a great idea. We're going to see a movie tonight. So thanks."

I shrug. "For what it's worth."

He nods and bumps my shoulder. "Good luck."

He and Ryan drift ahead, bobbing along with the mass of students making its way to the gym.

Good luck?

Suddenly I'm nervous. The Oracle isn't going to come up in the assembly, is it?

I find a seat at the edge of the center row of bleachers. I'm used to the stares by now. I'm surprised, however, when a few people pat me on the shoulder as they make their way up toward the higher rows.

I spot Kamryn sitting in a different set of bleachers. She's surrounded by a tight group of whispering girls. Her eyes are small and mean. I look away before they find me.

Ms. Parhar waits at the front of the gym until everyone has arrived.

When the shuffling subsides, she moves behind the podium and clears her throat. Her bracelets make ringing noises as she reaches for the mic.

"LaMontagne, thank you for your presence today," she starts. She runs through major announcements, and then the grade reps make theirs. Sports meet information. Spring fair. Then the dance team wraps it up with an awesome performance. They've put some sort of freak hip-hop king inside the mascot's costume today. The team does a great job, but Lucky the mascot steals the show. Jaws drop to see the pudgy panda popping and locking his way through Snoop Dogg. By the end of the performance, LaMontagne's student body is on its feet, cheering and clapping. The cheers turn to wild whoops when Lucky takes his head off to reveal tiny grade-ten student Lo Ming—a total nobody. She's panting, and her wet hair is stuck to her head. I imagine she's beat after five minutes of breaking inside fifteen pounds of polyester.

"Thanks to the dance team for that performance," says Ms. Parhar once the excitement has died down and everyone has found their seats again. "I've never seen our hundred-and-eight-year-old mascot move in quite such a way." Laughter ripples through the crowd and people glance in Lo Ming's direction. She bobs her head once in acknowledgment. One of the dance team pats her back.

She's not going to be a nobody anymore.

That's the funny thing. All it takes is one notable deed, and everlasting notoriety is yours.

Whether you want it or not.

"The final item on today's agenda concerns an issue that has been brought to my attention by one of LaMontagne's middle-school students," says Ms. Parhar.

"It involves enough of the student body that the staff felt it was appropriate to address at an assembly." As she speaks, the gym falls quiet. The usual foot-shuffling and whispering slows until it stops entirely.

I feel eyes on me. Dozens.

Maybe hundreds.

Is this about me?

I don't dare look toward the principal. I lock my eyes on the head of the person in front of me. I wait for her skull to start smoking.

"A blog has been brought to our attention. It appears that this website is attempting to mislead others in the area of personal relationships."

My stomach drops.

This *is* about the Oracle.

Chapter Thirteen

A rush of whispers breaks out as people speculate about who squealed.

"These are very serious charges," says Ms. Parhar. "The word *fraud* has been suggested."

The whispers swell to shocked murmurs.

My head suddenly feels too light. There's a squeezing sensation at the back of my brain. Fraud? That's punishable by time in jail. Surely I haven't done anything so bad?

Hannah's words come back to me. *You could get in big trouble if this ever gets out, Owen.*

"Without getting overly involved in an issue we as a staff know little about," Ms. Parhar continues, "we thought it would be best to invite the Oracle's administrator, Owen Roberts, to address these charges against him. And then we'll open the floor to other LaMontagne students. Owen?" Ms. Parhar scans the audience.

Somehow my legs stand me up. All around me, people are talking. No one is bothering to whisper. I'm glad. It's much easier to walk for twenty seconds through a hubbub than through pin-drop silence when everyone's eyes are on you.

I feel like I'm not even inside my body as I walk toward the front of the gym. I just kind of float there.

No one knows who ratted. Except for me.

And Hannah can probably guess.

I search her out among the grade eights. Our eyes meet, but then she looks away. I shouldn't be surprised.

I built this fire. And I'm going to burn alone.

My eyes travel back to Kamryn. She's sitting straight-backed on the bench with her arms folded tightly across her chest. A sour little smile plays across her face.

And then I'm standing beside Ms. Parhar. She steps to the side so I can stand behind the microphone. Everyone watches me, and it's quiet again. They expect something.

I swallow.

I'm glad I made a pit stop in the john just before break.

I lean into the mic and say exactly that, because I can't think of anything else.

The whole school erupts into laughter, and I feel myself relax. A lot of people are smiling. I pull my courage from them and start.

"I don't really have a lot to say," I say.

"That's a first!" someone calls. More laughter.

I smile. "I'll just tell you the truth. This is already as embarrassing as it could possibly get anyway. I started the Oracle for my own purposes," I say. "I wanted to, uh, I wanted to show someone I liked them." I clear my throat. "And I guess I was too shy to tell her in person, so I set up a blog to trick her into liking me."

Someone sets up a wolf whistle, and a few laughs drift toward me.

"Anyway, that plan backfired," I say. "I embarrassed her and hurt her feelings, and I feel really bad about that."

A group of grade-six girls sets up a little chorus of "*awwwwww*," and everyone laughs again.

I look over at Kamryn. I'm sure she'll want to kill me for identifying her, but I'm willing to take the risk. She's already called me out. I don't have anything else to lose.

"I'm sorry," I say to her. "I really am. It was a dumb thing to do."

Faces turn in Kamryn's direction. She stares stonily ahead, ignoring them. I'm sure this isn't what she had in mind.

"And I'm sorry to everyone else," I say. "Because I guess I tricked you too. Into thinking that the Oracle was a trustworthy site for advice." I drop my eyes to the floor. It's too hard to look into people's faces when I'm admitting what a mess I've made.

The murmurs start up again.

"Wait." A voice rises above all the others. "I want to say something." I look up to see Hannah picking her way down her row.

Ms. Parhar leans back toward the mic to introduce the next speaker.

"Hannah Cho, president of our middle-school student council, would like to have a few words."

Hannah jumps down from the stairs and walks briskly across the gym floor to stand beside me. She reaches up and pulls the mic off the stand. She's used to talking to a gym full of people.

"I've watched the Oracle grow from the start," Hannah says. "And I know for a fact that Owen took every question seriously. He worked hard to figure out the best answer for each person who wrote in."

I stare. This was the last thing I expected from Hannah.

"He stayed up late a lot of times so he could finish answering questions. He used more than one source when he put together his answers. He did an amazing job." She takes a deep breath. "And if you're wondering how I know all this... it's because I helped him."

Okay, correction. *This* was the last thing I expected from Hannah.

Gasps and chatter erupt from the group. Hannah Cho? Involved in a hoax?

"And this thing about it being fraud is ridiculous," she says, fixing Kamryn with a glare. "I mean, yes, Owen put himself out there as the Oracle, but he also wrote a disclaimer on the About page." She turns to Ms. Parhar. "It says very clearly that all of the Oracle's predictions are for entertainment purposes only." She looks back at the student body. "And besides, I think the Oracle did a lot more to help people than it did to hurt them. The Oracle—or should I say, Owen—has done more than just tell people how to be in love. What about *Always Angry*? And *Deeply Depressed*? What about *Losing Hope*?"

People are nodding. Some students look around, craning their necks to see whether anyone might suddenly give away their identity as one of those writers. But nobody does.

I think of *Losing Hope*. I wonder if she's okay.

"The Oracle took those students' concerns seriously, didn't he?" Hannah continues.

More murmurs. Nods.

Hannah looks around. "The Oracle did so much more than just give people good pickup lines."

This gets a few chuckles.

Jon throws me a thumbs-up, and I grin. *Rubber Duckie*, indeed.

"It's run by a guy who has proven that he can be trusted. Think about it, people. Owen Roberts is in possession of some of the biggest secrets among this school's population. But has he betrayed your trust on any of them?" Hannah has a way of speaking in public that's very much like a politician.

Several shouts. "No!"

"Has the Oracle ever led you astray?"

"NO!" More voices that time.

"Can you trust the Oracle? I ask you, can you place your trust in Owen Roberts?" As she speaks, Hannah extends her arm in my direction. She's whipping the crowd into a frenzy.

"YES!" Clapping. A whistle.

"I just want to add one more thing," Hannah says when the noise dies down. "I know for a fact that a number of relationships have gotten started because of the Oracle's advice."

Someone whistles again. Down near the front, a grade-eleven guy hoots and grabs the hand of the girl sitting next to him. He raises it into the air triumphantly. She blushes and smiles and tries to pull her hand away.

"See?" Hannah says. She crosses the stage and extends her other arm toward me. "Ladies and gentlemen," she says, "I give you...Owen Roberts, LaMontagne's *very own Oracle!*"

I laugh and shake my head as the applause starts.

Soon the whole gym is filled with the sound of applause. I look to the side and see the teachers—dozens of teachers—clapping or nodding or smiling.

And then.

I can hardly believe my eyes.

In ones and twos, people start to stand. They're still clapping, and they're smiling. They look at me and look around at each other and cheer. A deep thrumming rises from the bleachers, and it takes me a few seconds to realize that people are stomping too.

While the ovation is still going strong—except for Kamryn and her friends, who are pretty much the only people left sitting in the whole gym—Hannah gives a brief bow.

Then she turns and gives me a smile that makes my stomach flip right over.

She puts the microphone back on its stand, nods to Ms. Parhar and returns to her seat.

The principal waits for the noise to die away. "Thank you, Hannah. Well spoken, as always." She turns to me. "When the complaint was initially lodged against the Oracle, Owen," she says, "I did take the time to read many of the questions and answers on the website. And I have to say, I was impressed with the quality of advice the Oracle was providing."

I acknowledge her words with a nod.

Man, dailyhoroscope.com really saved my butt.

"Given the positive reaction we have witnessed today," Ms. Parhar continues, nodding her head toward the bleachers, "it seems you have earned the general approval of your peers." She looks toward the teachers. "And I, for one, have no intention of asking you to stop."

More applause.

I lean on the lectern and speak into the mic. "Thanks, Ms. Parhar," I say. "Thank you, too, Hannah. And thanks to everyone else." A few people whistle.

"One last thing, Owen," says the principal. "Since you're the only one who can predict the future, I'm going to ask you the question that's on everyone's mind right now." She looks around at the crowd, then back at me. "Are you going to continue with the Oracle?"

I close my eyes as though I'm meditating. I raise my hands and press my palms against my temples for dramatic effect. There are a few snickers, then the gym grows quiet waiting for my response.

"As I see it," I begin, and then I open my eyes, "I'm gonna start charging a hundred bucks a pop!"

The gym erupts into laughter.

I look for Hannah.

She's smiling.

Acknowledgments

My thanks, as always, to the wonderful people at Orca Book Publishers. You are an excellent team to work with. Special thanks to editor Melanie Jeffs for her suggestions and guidance in smoothing *Oracle*'s rough edges.

Alex Van Tol taught middle school for eight years, then made the switch to writing for a living. She has published numerous titles with Orca Book Publishers. *Oracle* is her first Orca Currents novel. Alex lives in Victoria, British Columbia, with her two sons, who are still too little to figure out how to start and maintain fraudulent blogs.

Titles in the Series

orca currents

orca currents

For more information on all the books
in the Orca Currents series, please visit
www.orcabook.com